How to
Get Rid of
Ghosts

How to Get Rid of Ghosts

Catherine Leblanc

Roland Garrigue

INSIGHT KIDS

San Rafael, California

Ghosts can float straight through walls
and enter any room, even when every door is locked . . .
but they get caught in sticky spider webs.
Weave great big webs all around the house to trap them!

When ghosts appear in a room,
the temperature drops suddenly.
And ice forms on the windowpanes!

To stop from shaking and shivering,
heat up a cup of piping hot chocolate—they hate that smell!

At night, ghosts make unsettling noises:

doors groan, ceilings tremble,

shutters clap, and floorboards creak.

Be brave! Grab a flashlight and run up to the attic.

The sight of a kid will make them shriek!

Ghosts float light in the air
but sink when they're **wet**!

Paddle about in your tub and relax.
Even with a floatie, they're too scared to swim!
Splash them and they'll rush to dry off!

Ghosts can move things without anyone noticing.
You'll find the sponge in a pot, a hat in the fridge,
and the table flipped with four legs in the air!

If a gang of little ghosts dumps all your sister's junk
in your room, don't take the blame. Say it wasn't you!

Ghosts love to mess with your alarm clock
to make you late for school!

They can make certain objects totally disappear.
Don't bother searching, they can't be found here!

Ghosts don't reflect in mirrors.

They can sneak up and tangle your hair while you're trying to comb.

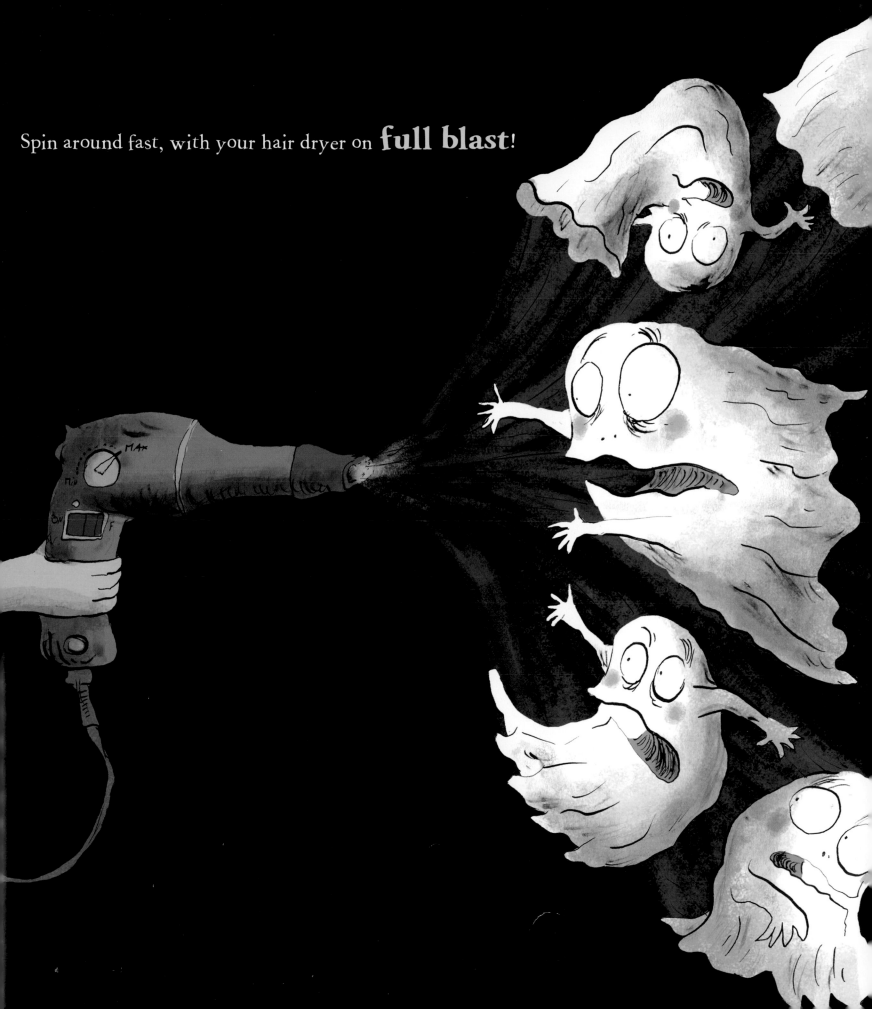

Spin around fast, with your hair dryer on **full blast**!

Ghosts have the power to erase your books,
leaving the pages completely white.

Only bright ink can resist their touch!
To save your favorite books,
highlight the pictures and words with your brightest red pen!

Some ghosts drag around a ball and chain.

Challenge them to a soccer game!
They won't score a single goal, but they'll get sweaty and worn out!

Ghosts love to follow us around, here and there. . . .

But they hate it when you sneeze, ACHOo!
And use them as a tissue!

Kitty-cat ghosts purr at your feet,
doggy ghosts lay their head in your lap,
and hamster ghosts nibble at your pillow.

All they want is to cozy up, but then your bed gets too crowded!
Shake your sheet as though it were the ghost of an
enormous tiger, ready to pounce on them!

But beware! If you get rid of all the ghosts, you might regret it. . . .

They take with them many mysteries and dreams.

And at night, no one will be there to tickle your feet!

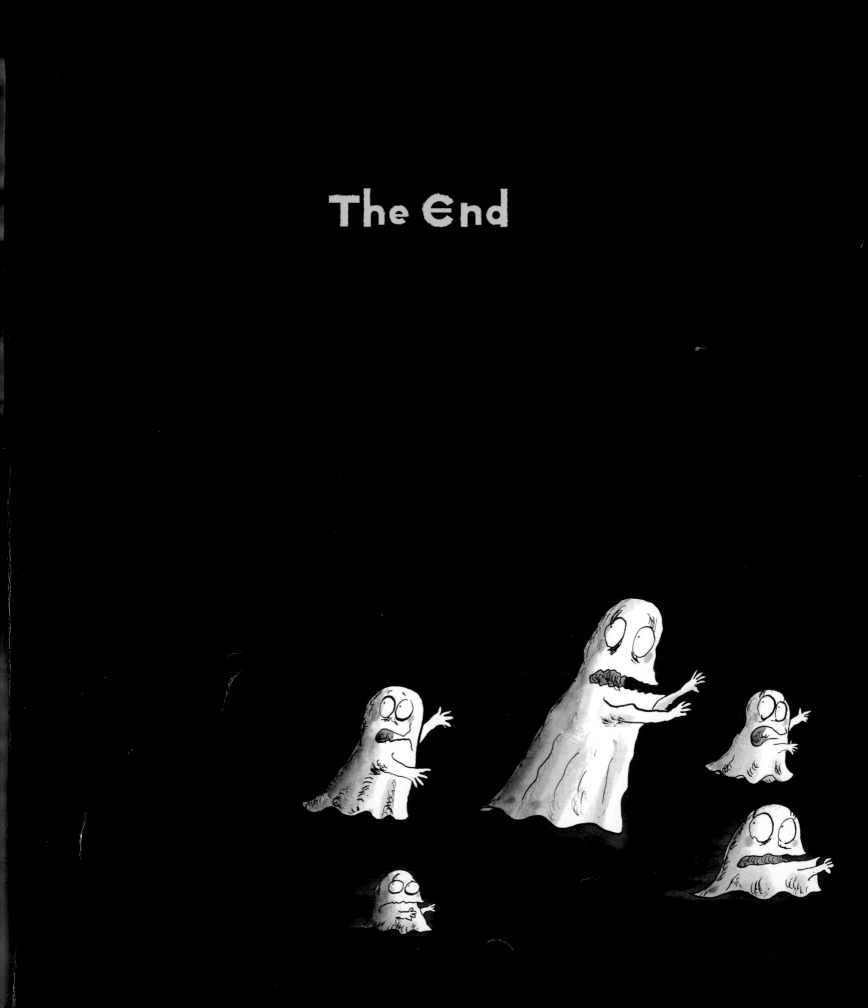

Once again, for my little girls, Louanne and Clémence, and for all
the children I meet, eager to hunt down ghosts.
—CL

To the little ghost hiding in my bathroom closet.
—RG

INSIGHT
KIDS

PO Box 3088
San Rafael, CA 94912
www.insighteditions.com

Find us on Facebook: www.facebook.com/InsightEditions
Follow us on Twitter: @insighteditions

First published in the United States in 2013 by Insight Editions.
Originally published in France in 2010 by Éditions Glénat.
Comment Ratatiner les Fantômes?
by C. Leblanc and R. Garrigue © 2010 Éditions Glénat
Translation © 2013 Insight Editions

Thanks to Christopher Goff and Marie Goff-Tuttle
for their help in translating this book.

Library of Congress Cataloging-in-Publication Data available.

ISBN: 978-1-60887-195-7

ROOTS of PEACE   REPLANTED PAPER

Insight Editions, in association with Roots of Peace, will plant two trees for each tree used in the
manufacturing of this book. Roots of Peace is an internationally renowned humanitarian organization
dedicated to eradicating land mines worldwide and converting war-torn lands into productive farms
and wildlife habitats. Roots of Peace will plant two million fruit and nut trees in Afghanistan and
provide farmers there with the skills and support necessary for sustainable land use.

Manufactured in China by Insight Editions

10 9 8 7 6 5 4 3 2 1